Back in the day... the captain and his boy.

D1605536

Be brave & Enjoy your journey

Timothy A. Weeks   David D. Weeks

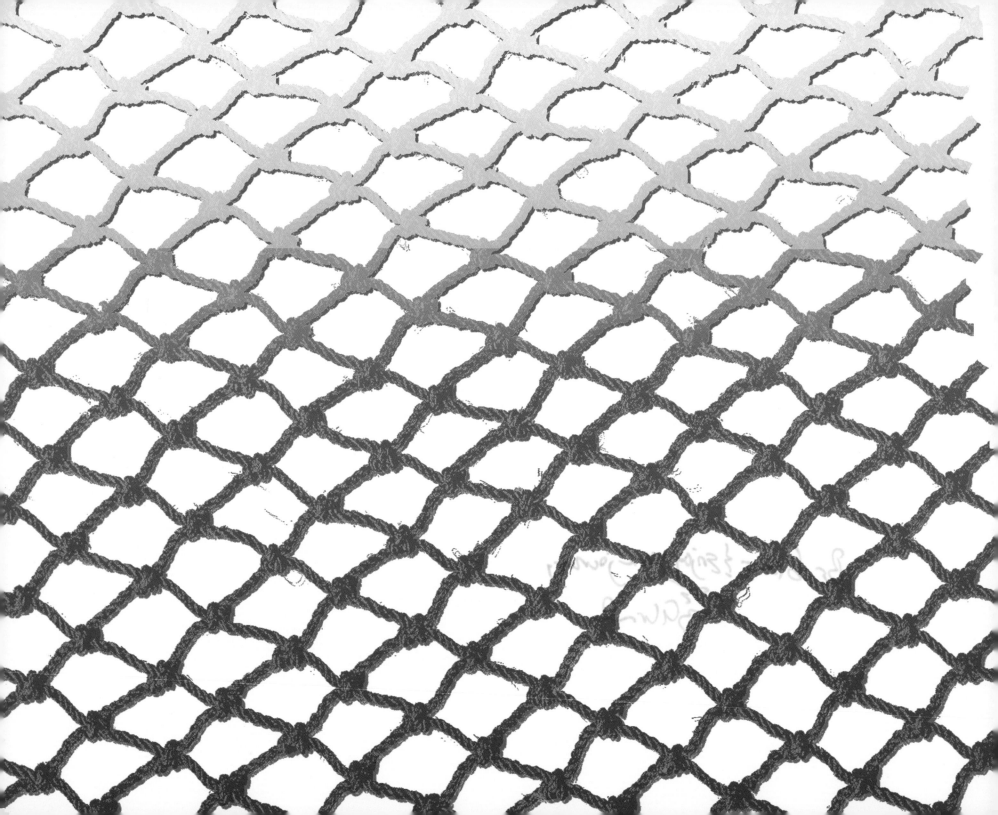

This Book Belongs To:

_____

_____
From

_____
Date

DEDICATED TO

Scott Hart Kennedy

(The Little Prince who felt Everything)

Author Timothy A. Weeks
watches while Scott releases
his catch back into East Bay.

-Summer 2003

AND TO THE CAPTAIN WHO TOOK ME FISHING.

David D. Weeks

Timothy and his Papa enjoying a good day of mullet fishing in Cook Bayou.

-Summer 1980

The Wise Mullet of Cook Bayou

Written by

Timothy A. Weeks

Based on an old fable by the Venerable Rumi

Illustrator: Miss Jeanne
Digital Graphics: Tim Thomas
Editor: Kimberlee S. Bryant

ISBN 0-9779928-0-2   Revised First Edition
Published by Foolosophy Media 2006
SAN # 850-8186
Copyright 2004 Timothy A. Weeks

First published in 2004 by Thomas Expressions

All rights reserved. No part of this book shall be reproduced, stored in a retrieval
system, or transmitted by any means without written permission from the author.

Direct queries to:
Foolosophy Media
1528 Primrose Lane, Panama City, Florida, 32404
(850) 871-2304/819-5623
wisemullet@gmail.com

Printed in the United States of America
by BookMasters

The Wise Mullet of Cook Bayou

Written by

Timothy A. Weeks

Based on an old fable by the Venerable Rumi

Once upon a time in the muddy waters of Cook Bayou, there lived three mullet:

One wise, one middling, and one as dumb as the mud he ate every day for breakfast.

Together they grew up as best mates—
Far, far away from everything,
but not far enough.

For one day a boat idled into the bayou.
It was a boy and his Papa fishing.

Hearing the sound of the motor, the wise mullet grew wary. And when he saw the name written on the boat and the big net piled up on the back deck, he said, "Mates, we've got to skeedaddle!"

"But where?" wondered the middling mullet, who never could decide what to do. "But why?" asked the dumb mullet, who was scared of change and wanted his *todays* to be just like his *yesterdays*.

Now normally the wise mullet was patient with his sluggish friends and their tardy ways,

because he had a golden tongue that could always convince them to follow him anywhere. But today was not a day to ask *But where?* and *But why?*, but a day to *think swift* and *act swifter*.

A little voice told the wise mullet that it was time to get busy paddling his black fins instead of wagging his golden tongue.

So off he high-tailed around the end of the net, just before the boy could drag it to the beach and trap him inside.

Inside the net his two mates
remained, watching in horror
as the boy and his Papa pulled
the net closer and closer together.

"What a fool I was to hesitate,"
the middling mullet said to himself.
"Next time, I won't wait until it's too late."

But as the net came closer and closer, he realized that there wasn't going to be a next time. His fate was sealed by the net. He fainted from the fear of his approaching doom and floated to the top of the water. The boy proudly grabbed the floating mullet and held him up high, but his Papa tossed the mullet aside saying, "Son, we don't eat fish that are already dead."

The middling mullet landed with a crash in the bulrushes that grew around the edge of the bayou. Waking up, he flounced desperately about, unable to breathe out of the water.

This time he did not give up or faint with fear, and finally the middling mullet flipped into the water and swam away.

The boy's Mama expertly cooked the fish golden brown. Then the boy joyfully picked the bones clean during a yummy family supper of fried mullet and cheese grits.

For the wise mullet the adventure was just beginning.
Fearing his mates had been captured in the net, he
left Cook Bayou and swam into the wide-open waters of East Bay,
which were full of bizarre creatures he had never before seen.

Sad, scared, and all alone, he kept moving, always on his guard.
In this strange new world of scary surprises, he quickly learned that
he had to do things differently than he did in Cook Bayou.

Here in the wide-open waters of East Bay, the old trusty ways didn't work. He had to adapt if he was ever to survive.

Fortunately, the wise mullet never forgot to listen to his little voice, which always, in the moment of trouble, would tell him what to do.

The mysterious thing was that the little voice always had a different solution to whatever trouble he faced.

Sometimes the little voice told him to swim around danger,

sometimes to jump over,

and other times, to remain perfectly still.

But every time he needed it the little voice came through,
as long as he listened and didn't panic.

This is how he became a wise mullet.
Not because of who he was or what he said, but how he acted.

For days and days and weeks and weeks he traveled:
Past tug boats pushing barges loaded with coal,

past smoking factories

and humongous ships,

under bridges full of honking cars
and beneath moonlit skies,

through stormy seas

WEST BAY

Pretty Bayou

He journeyed all the way from East Bay to West Bay.

Cook Bayou

EAST BAY

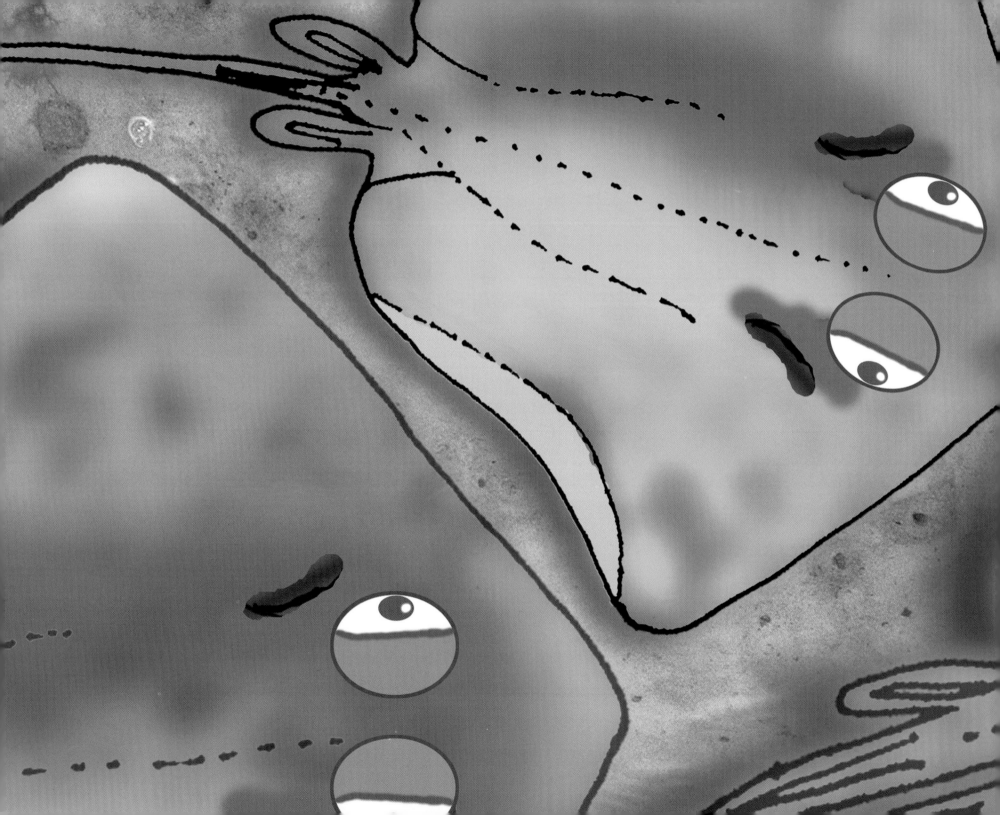

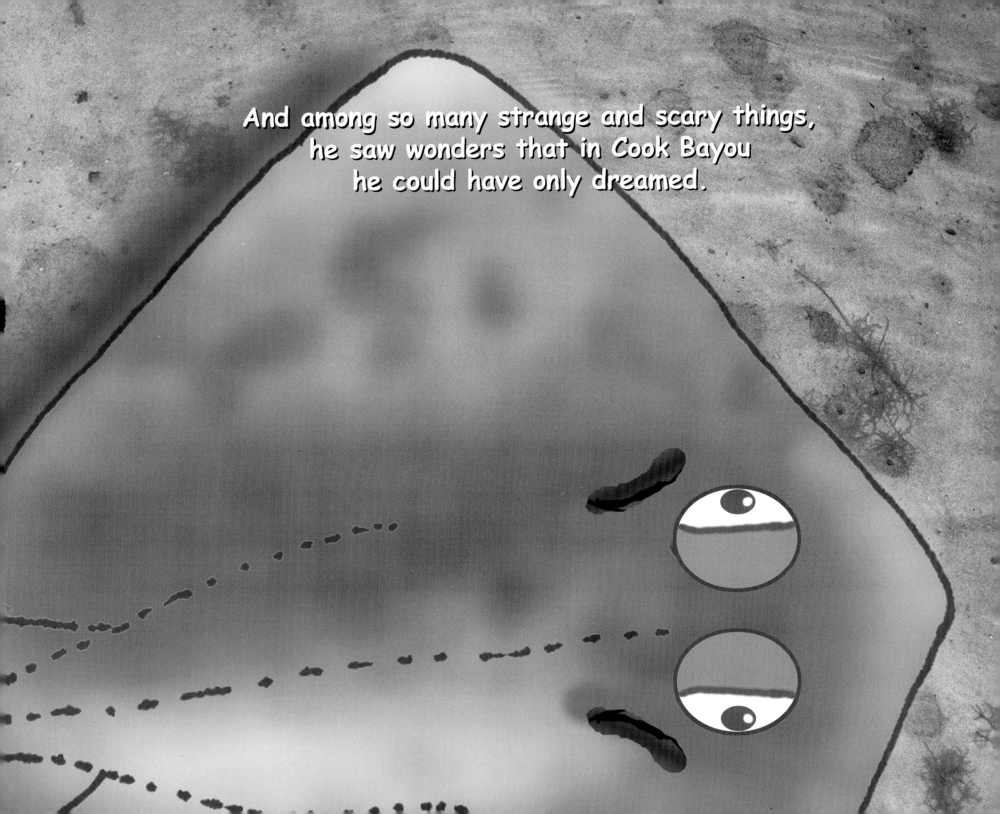

One fine day, on the sunny side of West Bay, he found a calm, beautiful bayou. In it lived a mullet with the shiniest scales he had ever seen.

"Where did you come from?" asked the mullet with the shiniest of scales.

"I came from Cook Bayou, through the wide-open waters of East Bay," the wise mullet said. "Where am I now?"

"You are in Pretty Bayou," she replied. "What brought you all the way from East Bay to West Bay?"

"A little voice," the wise mullet said. "What did it tell you?" she asked. "It told me when trouble knocks, don't answer the door."

As time passed, the wise mullet with the golden tongue and this mullet with the shiniest of scales became dazzling friends.

Together they played the mullet's favorite game, which is to jump out of the water and see who can make the biggest splash.

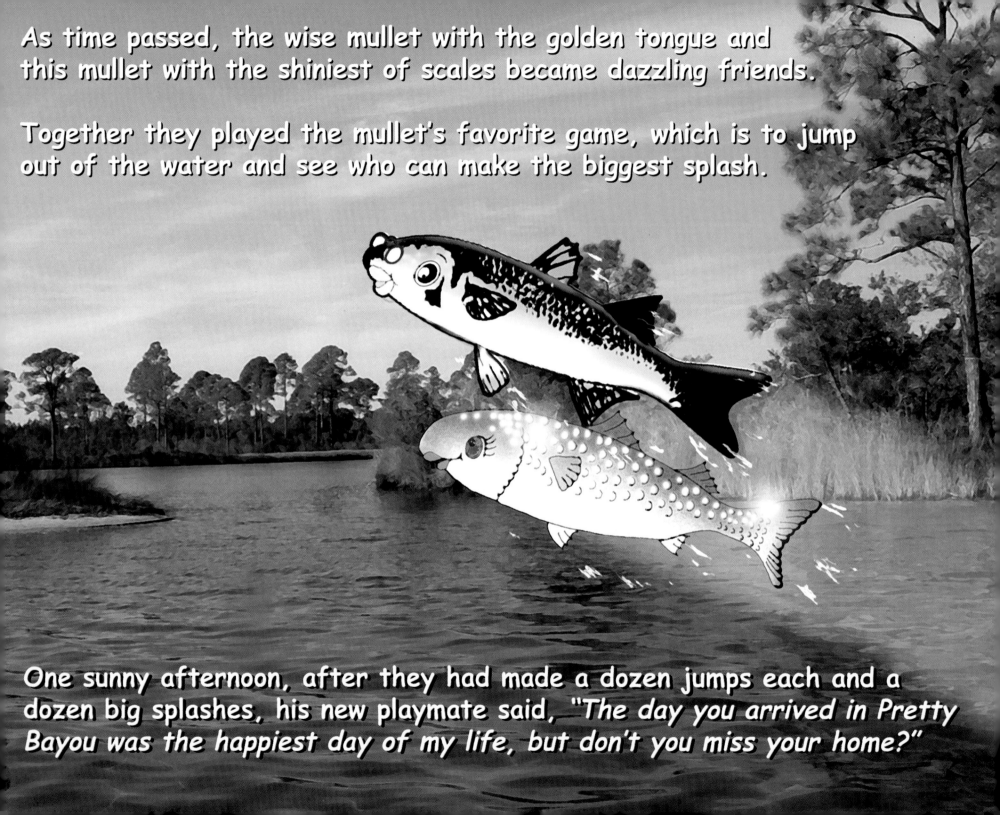

One sunny afternoon, after they had made a dozen jumps each and a dozen big splashes, his new playmate said, *"The day you arrived in Pretty Bayou was the happiest day of my life, but don't you miss your home?"*

The wise mullet looked around. He liked this Pretty Bayou, even if it had a funny name. There was plenty of mud to eat and plenty of room to play and plenty of places to hide should danger come. He also fancied this playful mullet and her shiny scales very much. "No," the wise mullet replied, "I don't miss home, because home is not only where you come from or where you are, but where you're heading."

The Mullet Family (mugilidae)

Black Mullet (Striped)-mugil cephalus
Silver Mullet-mugil curema

Their distinctive shape and coloring, along with two separate dorsal fins, make the mullet fish easy to identify. They have short, rounded heads, silver bodies and white bellies. Silver mullet are lighter on top than black mullet. Their tails are edged in black so that they appear in water to be marked with a black "V". The tails of black mullet are dark all over. Typically, mullet will grow to about a foot and a half in length and weigh about two pounds.

Mullet are primarily vegetarian. They feed by digging headfirst into the mud and swinging their heads back and forth. This action kicks up organic detritus (edible bottom material) and small, mud-dwelling organisms. These are sifted through the bristly, nearly invisible teeth in their triangle-shaped mouth and strainer-like gills. Mullet have a highly modified stomach known as a gizzard that acts like a grinding mill for their food.

Black mullet spawn in autumn in deep waters offshore. Once hatched, the young make their way into shallow bays, rivers, lagoons and bayous. Like most silvery fish, mullet travel in schools. They can be found worldwide in warmer waters. Fishermen use cast nets and gill nets to catch mullet, but these fish are great jumpers, leaping out of the water to avoid nets and predators, and for the sheer joy of it. Jumping is simply the nature of the fish.

Long an important source of food, mullet have a high oil content that makes them tastier if eaten fresh. The ancient Romans ate them; modern Italians still do. Besides those coming from the muddy waters of Cook Bayou, author Timothy A. Weeks has eaten mullet caught off the shores of France, Italy, Thailand and The Netherlands.

A journalist based in Amsterdam, The Netherlands, Timothy A. Weeks spent the first part of his life chasing mullet, the second chasing rainbows, and plans on spending the remainder of his days spinning yarns about these pursuits.

Growing up in Cook Bayou, Kimberlee Bryant, was frequently seen with war wounds from pinecone fights and tree climbing. Now healed, she lives with her husband, Enoch, and son, Beau David, in North Pole, Alaska, where she is a supervisor in adult education.

Jeanne Weeks is not only the proud mother of both Timothy and Kimberlee, but also the book's illustrator. Retiring after 21 years as the owner of a daycare, Miss Jeanne resides in the Cook Bayou area of Panama City, Florida, with her husband Captain David.

Tim Thomas is the owner of a graphics studio and self-publishing company in Panama City, Florida. He is the author/illustrator of various children's books. Tim also resides in the Cook Bayou area with his wife, Terri, and son, Tanis.

Special Souls from the Bayou

To Johnny Davis, for keeping his net wet,
& jovial Mr. Pilcher, for supplying the bait.

To Mama Stubbs' morning waves when the night's
fishing was done,
To Harry's paying tribute to those who have gone on.

To Mildon's blueberries, Sue's brownies,
& the flavor that they gave.

To cultural desserts topped with Huey's wit,
To Gloria's roast beef & her Christ-like tact,
& the Kennedy sisters for spit-polishing my act.

To little Scott's daddy, Warren, the Great Noble Hunter,
& my buddy Benjamin, the lovable one.

To the pioneering James Poston, gentle Myrtis,
& their catfish pond,
To the lost boys of East Bay,
& all my elders who have headed to their final home.

To Bo, swatting my 9-year-old fastballs deep into left field,
& to Jerry's lonely motorcycle, gathering dust on its wheels.

To Cornbread, Aileen & Pat the Diamond.
To Granny Anders, a true millionaire if ever there was one.

To the always-open dock of merry Mr. Menge,
& to Sylvia Byrd for being a best friend to Miss Jeanne.

To the sweetness of Miss Pitts' scuppernong grapes,
& all the roughhousing ruffians in Wednesday RAs.

To Fran Dean's laugh & Paul Ryals' handshake,
To my dear playmate Anna Lea.

To my Captain, King David, a Great Fisher of Fish & Men,
& queenly Miss Jeanne, who loved & loved & loved 'tis true,
& the world's finest chicken trainer – my favorite Kimbie Sue.

To Gayle for trying to shine my shoeless soul,
& Bobby's time for every sport in season.

To Reverend George & Gracie,
To Reverend Gene & Jackie,
Who fed Cook Bayou's hungry with their kindly Christian ways.

To the sounds of the organ & Linda's heavenly smile,
& *A Mighty Fortress* booming from Ed Johnson's pew,
To the choir's glorious noise made unto the Lord,
& Wayne directing it straight through the roof.

To the Flowing Well.
To everyone that shared my mullet & bought my eggs.

To all the good folks who have graced the banks of Cook Bayou,
& to the muddy waters of Cook Bayou itself, which fed me,
tested me & bore me up.

& finally, to James Curtis Melvin, Budroe Davis,
& all the *Mullet Masters* who are no more...

Miss Jeanne's
(Nearly World Famous)
Cheese Grits Recipe

4 cups water
½ tsp. salt (optional)
1 tsp. butter
1-1¼ cups grits
¾-1 cup soft cheese

Bring water and salt to a boil. Stir in grits and cook slowly 5-6 minutes.
Add butter and cheese. Stir and serve. Enjoy!

Golden Brown Mullet

Remove scales by scraping the mullet. Cut fish into filets or frying-size pieces.
Wash filets or pieces and sprinkle with seafood seasoning or salt and pepper.
Coat each with flour or cornmeal. Add peanut oil to frying pan deep enough to almost cover fish.
Heat to frying temperature. Add fish carefully to hot oil.
Cook to golden brown on both sides. Yum yum!

Fried Mullet and Cheese Grits is an old Southern favorite, and a staple among Cook Bayou residents.
I hope you and your family will enjoy this meal as much as we have over the years!

-Miss Jeanne